Andres an Rubik's Cube MADNESS

by Andrea Alvarez

Illustrated by Ana Sebastian

Andrea Alvarez
Jan. 2020

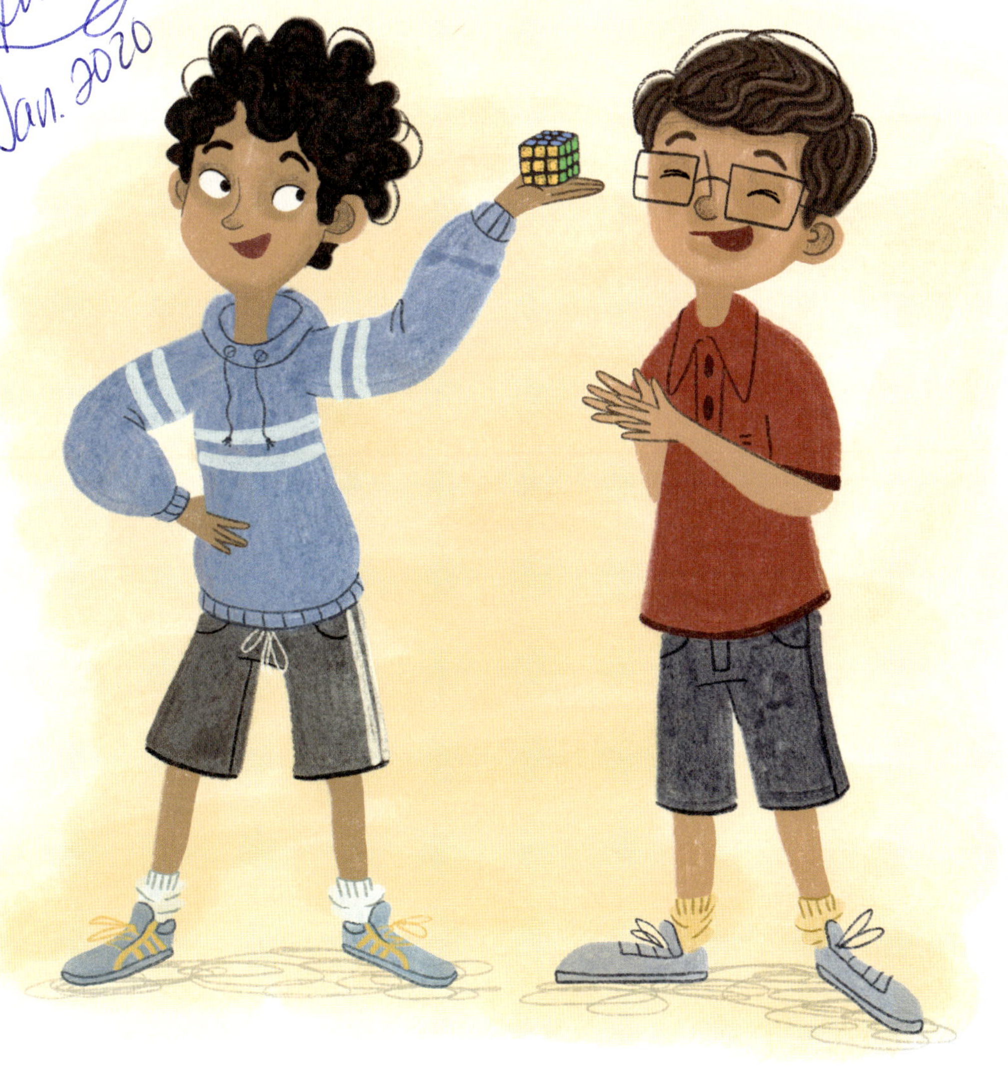

Andres heard kids chattering outside his house. Curious, he went out and saw his friends surrounding the new kid in the neighborhood. Kino was solving a Rubik's cube SUPER fast.

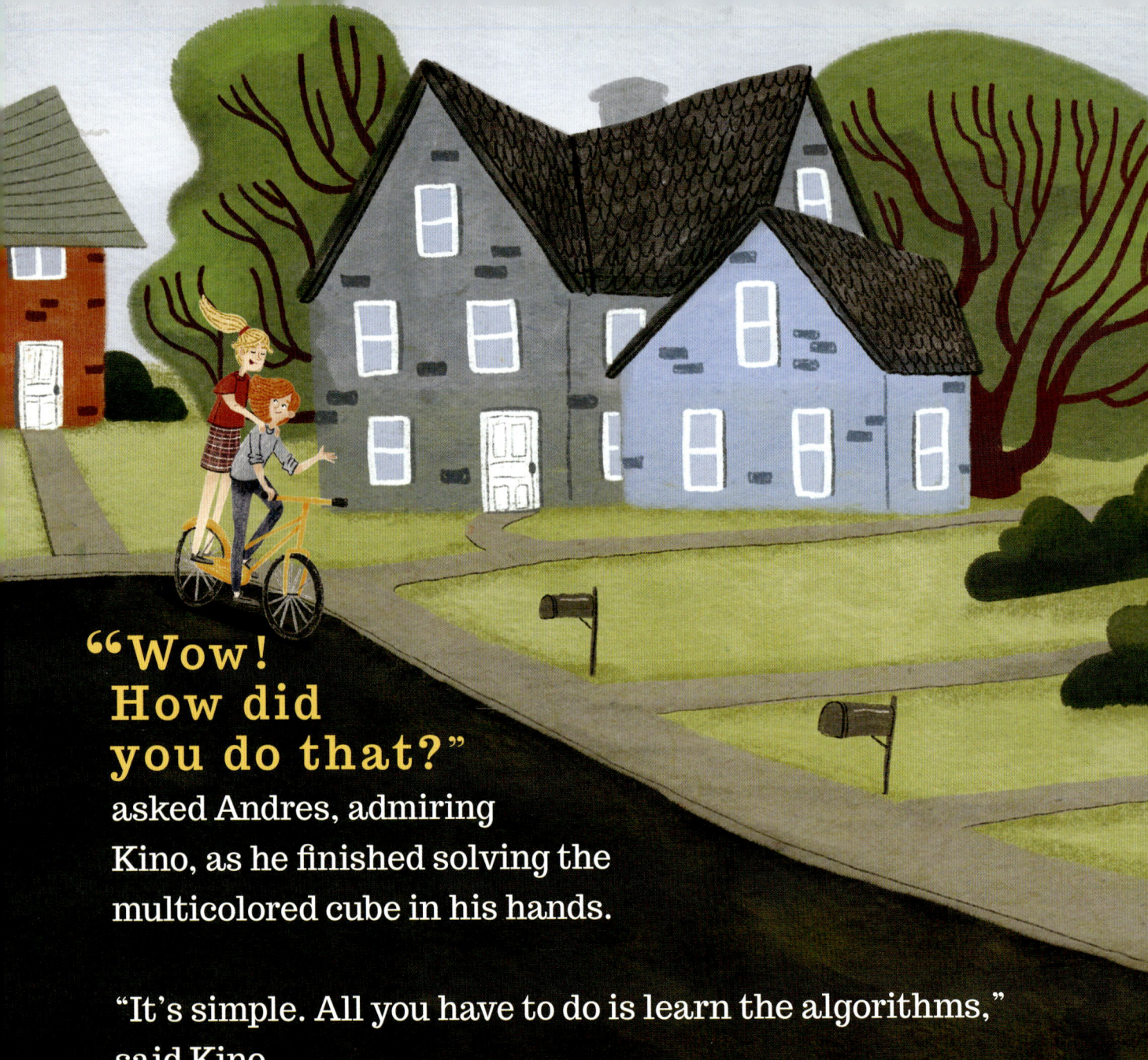

"**Wow! How did you do that?**" asked Andres, admiring Kino, as he finished solving the multicolored cube in his hands.

"It's simple. All you have to do is learn the algorithms," said Kino.

"The what?! What are al-go-rithms?" asked Andres. "Algorithms are like math codes. The more you memorize, the easier it is to solve the cube."

Andres had no idea what Kino was talking about, but it sounded fun. "Can I try it?"

Kino handed over the Rubik's cube. Andres twisted it in different directions, trying to get all the faces to be one color. He tried again and again, but the colors were more mixed up than before. "This is impossible!" Andres yelled.

"It's not," Kino laughed, "but it takes time to learn."

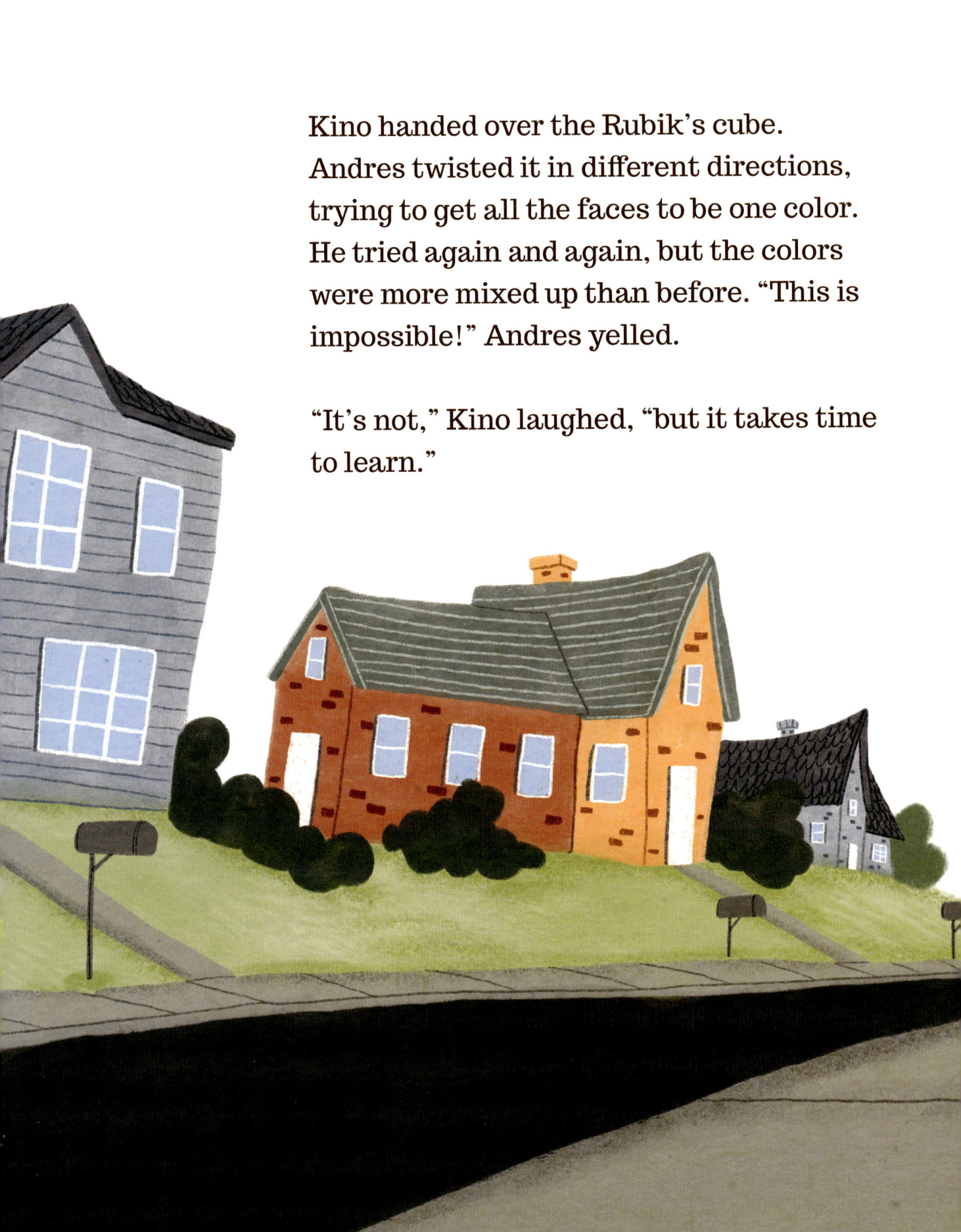

At home, Andres told his mom all about Kino.

"What if I can learn too?" asked Andres.

"You can do anything you set your mind to," she said, "but you must work hard."

Andres thought about this and realized he could do it too. Determined to learn, his mom bought him his first Rubik's cube.

From that day on, Andres took the Rubik's cube everywhere he went.

He practiced at **home**...

during **car rides**...

on his bed...

and even in his sleep.

It was madness!

One day, after a lot of practice, THERE IT WAS! Red, white, blue, green, orange, and yellow, all solved on each side.

"Mom! Mom!" Andres shouted. "I solved it! I solved the Rubik's cube!"

"I knew you could!" she said with a big smile as she pulled him in close and hugged him.

But Andres didn't stop there. He wanted to solve it again, and faster.

So, Andres worked and worked until he memorized as many algorithms as he could. He wrote them down and practiced one by one.

And as he continued to learn, he discovered that Rubik's cube competitions are held all over the world.

Kids EVERYWHERE competed.

and Australia...

Even in Antarctica, the coldest place on Earth!

Then, a daring idea popped into his head.

"What if I could compete too?"

Andres imagined himself competing at the biggest Rubik's cube championship. But to qualify, he would have to first compete and solve the Rubik's cube in 35 seconds or less.

He thought about this but not for long. Because Andres knew...he had to try!

During the next few days, Andres practiced so much that his hands hurt. Sometimes, when twisting the cube, the pieces would pop and fall apart. "Oh, no!" he cried. But every time, Andres put the pieces together again and practiced some more.

Andres showed Kino his progress. "Wow, 28 seconds!" Kino exclaimed. "You learned fast!"

"It's fun!" said Andres. "Come on, let's solve some cubes."

Kino and Andres quickly became friends and together they practiced until the day of the competition arrived.

On the day of the competition, Andres was nervous. What if he didn't solve the Rubik's cube fast enough to qualify? He looked around and saw that everyone was there to support him—mom, dad, grandma, his cousin Jonie, Kino, and even his dog, Leo.

The announcer called his name. Andres confidently walked to the stage and smiled.

He took a deep breath, grabbed the unsolved Rubik's cube, and began twisting it quickly.

The timer started ticking...

"Done!"

Andres shouted. But was it fast enough?
He looked at the timer…

Fifteen seconds!

"Yes!" Andres cheered.

Everyone ran up to Andres and hugged him. "I qualified!" Andres yelled.

"You practiced every day," said his mom proudly, "but most importantly, you NEVER gave up."

Andres was thrilled. But the happiness he felt in that very moment, surrounded by his family, was the best feeling of it all.

His dream of competing at the biggest championship became true.

Andres didn't know if he would win, but he knew one thing...

He was ready to try!

AUTHOR'S NOTE

Dear Reader:

Did you know that the fastest Rubik's cube solve is under four seconds? Pretty fast, right? And did you know that less than six percent of the world's population can solve a Rubik's cube?

In recent years, the Rubik's cube puzzle has become more popular due to the large number of competitions worldwide. To win, the speed-cuber must solve the cube five times in the final event and average the fastest result, excluding the fastest and slowest time.

For Andres, learning to solve the Rubik's cube was a fun challenge. Andres worked hard every day to learn to solve it, but once he finally learned, no one could stop him. After three months of practice, Andres' first official solve was 50.94 seconds. Since then, he's competed in multiple competitions and twice at the Cubing USA Nationals, where he's met some of the fastest speed-cubers in the world. Andres has reached an 8.33 second solve and has learned to solve different types of Rubik's cube puzzles, such as: the 2x2, 4x4, 5x5, the Pyraminx, Megaminx, Skewb, and others.

To learn more about Rubik's cube competitions, visit the World Cube Association website at worldcubeassociation.org